DEATH IS NOT THE END

Also by Ian Rankin

DEATH IS NOT THE END

An Inspector Rebus Novella

Ian Rankin

St. Martin's Minotaur ❧ New York

ISBN 0-312-26142-X

First published in Great Britain by Orion Books Ltd

First St. Martin's Minotaur Edition: June 2000

10 9 8 7 6 5 4 3 2 1

ONE

Is loss redeemed by memory? Or does memory merely swell the sense of loss, becoming the enemy? The language of loss is the language of memory: remembrance, memorial, memento. People leave our lives all the time: some we met only briefly, others we'd known since birth. They leave us memories – which become skewed through time – and little more.

The silent dance continued. Couples writhed and shuffled, threw back their heads or ran hands through their hair, eyes darting around the dance floor, seeking out future partners maybe, or past loves to make jealous. The TV monitor gave a greasy look to everything.

No sound, just pictures, the tape cutting from dance floor to main bar to second bar to toilet hallway, then entrance foyer, exterior front and exterior back. Exterior back was a puddled alley, full of rubbish bins and a Merc belonging to the club's owner. Rebus had heard about the alley: a punter had been knifed there the previous summer. Mr Merc had complained about the bloody smear on his passenger-side window. The victim had lived.

The club was called Gaitanos, nobody knew why. The owner just said it sounded American and a bit jazzy. The larger part of the clientele had decided on the nickname 'Guisers', and that was what you heard in the pubs on a Friday and Saturday night – 'Going down Guisers later?' The young men would be dressed smart-casual, the women scented from heaven and all stations south. They left the pubs around ten or half past – that's when it would be starting to get lively at Guisers.

Rebus was seated in a small uncomfortable chair which itself sat in a stuffy dimly lit room. The other chair was filled by an audio-visual technician, armed with two remotes. His occasional belches – of which he seemed blissfully ignorant – bespoke a recent snack of spring onion crisps and Irn-Bru.

'I'm really only interested in the main bar, foyer and out front,' Rebus said.

'I could edit them down to another tape, but we'd lose definition. The recording's duff enough as it is.' The technician scratched inside the sagging armpit of his black T-shirt.

Rebus leant forward a little, pointing at the screen. 'Coming up now.' They waited. The view jumped from back alley to dance floor. 'Any second.' Another cut: main bar, punters queuing three deep. The technician didn't need to be told, and froze the picture. It wasn't so much black and white as sepia, the colour of dead photographs. Interior light, the audio-visual wizard had explained. He was adjusting the tracking now, and moving the action along one frame at a time. Rebus moved in on the screen, bending so one knee rested on the floor. His finger was touching a face. He took out the assortment of photos from his pocket and held them against the screen.

'It's him,' he said. 'I was pretty sure before. You can't go in a bit closer?'

'For now, this is as good as it gets. I can work on it later, stick it on the computer. The problem is the source material, to wit: one shitty security video.'

Rebus sat back on his chair. 'All right,' he said. 'Let's run forward at half-speed.'

The camera stayed with the main bar for another fifteen seconds, then switched to the second bar and all points on the compass. When it returned to the main bar, the crush of drinkers seemed not to have moved. Unbidden, the technician froze the tape again.

'He's not there,' Rebus said. Again he approached the screen, touched it with his finger. 'He should be there.'

'Next to the sex goddess.' The technician belched again.

Yes. Spun silver hair, almost like a cloud of candy-floss, dark eyes and lips. While those around her were intent either on catching the eyes of the bar staff or on the dance floor, she was looking off to one side. There were no shoulders to her dress.

'Let's check the foyer,' Rebus said.

Twenty seconds there showed a steady stream entering the club, but no one leaving. Exterior front showed a queue awaiting admittance by the brace of bouncers, and a few passers-by.

'In the toilet maybe,' the technician suggested. But Rebus had studied the tape a dozen times already, and though he watched just once more he knew he wouldn't see the young man again, not at the bar, not on the dance floor, and not back around the table where his mates were waiting – with increasing disbelief and impatience – for him to get his round in.

The young man's name was Damon Mee and, according to the timer running at the bottom right-hand corner of the screen, he had vanished from the world sometime between 11.44 and 11.45pm on Friday 22 April.

'Where is this place anyway? I don't recognize it.'

'Kirkcaldy,' Rebus said.

The technician looked at him. 'How come it ended up here?'

Good question, Rebus thought, but not one he was about to answer. 'Go back to that bar shot,' he said. 'Take it nice and slow again.'

The technician aimed his right-hand remote. 'Yes, sir, Mr DeMille,' he said.

April meant still not quite spring in Edinburgh. A few sunny days to be sure, buds getting twitchy, wondering if winter had been paid the ransom. But there was snow still hanging in a sky the colour of chicken bones. Office talk: how Rangers were going to retain the championship; why Hearts and Hibs would never win it – was it finally time for the two local sides to become friends, form one team which might – *might* – stand half a chance? As someone said, their rivalry was part and parcel of the city's make-up. Hard to imagine Rangers and Celtic thinking of marriage in the same way, or even of a quick poke on the back stairs.

After years of following football only on pub tele-visions and in the back of the daily tabloid, Rebus was starting to go to matches again. DC Siobhan Clarke was to blame, coaxing him to a Hibs game one dreary afternoon. The men on the green sward weren't half as interesting as the spectators, who proved by turns sharp-witted, vulgar, perceptive and incorrigible. Siobhan had taken him to her usual spot. Those in the vicinity seemed to know her pretty well. It was a good-humoured afternoon, even if Rebus couldn't have said who scored the eventual three goals. But Hibs had won: the final-whistle hug from Siobhan was proof of that.

It was interesting to Rebus that, for all the barriers around the ground, this was a place where shields were dropped. After a while, it felt like one of the safest places he'd ever been. He recalled fixtures his father had taken him to in the fifties and early sixties – Cowdenbeath home games, and a crowd numbered in the hundreds; getting there necessitated a change of buses, Rebus and his younger brother fighting over who could hold the roll of tickets. Their mother was dead by then and their father was trying to carry on much as before, like they might not notice she was missing. Those Saturday trips to the football were supposed to fill a gap. You saw a lot of fathers and sons on the terraces but not many mothers, and that in itself was reminder enough. There was a boy of Rebus's age who stood near them. Rebus had walked over to him one day and blurted out the truth.

'I don't have a mum at home.'

The boy had stared at him, saying nothing.

Ever since, football had reminded him of those days and of his mother. He stood on the terraces alone these days and followed the game mostly – movements which could be graceful as ballet or as jagged as free association – but sometimes found that he'd drifted elsewhere, to a place not at all unpleasant, and all the time surrounded by a community of bodies and wills.

'I'll tell you how to beat Rangers,' he said now, addressing the whole office.

'How?' Siobhan Clarke offered.

'Clone Stevie Scoular half a dozen times.'

There were murmurs of agreement, and then the Farmer put his head around the door.

'John, my office.'

The Farmer – Chief Superintendent Watson to his face – was pouring a mug of coffee from his machine when Rebus knocked at the open door.

'Sit down, John.' Rebus sat. The Farmer motioned with an empty mug, but he turned down the offer and waited for his boss to get to his chair and the point both.

'My birthday's coming up,' the Farmer said. This was a new one on Rebus, who kept quiet. 'I'd like a present.'

'Not just a card this year then?'

'What I want, John, is Topper Hamilton.'

Rebus let that sink in. 'I thought Topper was Mr Clean these days?'

'Not in my books.' The Farmer cupped his hands around his coffee mug. 'He got a fright last time and, granted, he's been keeping a low profile, but we both know the best villains have got little or no profile at all.'

'So what's he been up to?'

'I heard a story he's the sleeping partner in a couple of clubs and casinos. I also hear he bought a taxi firm from Big Ger Cafferty when Big Ger went into Barlinnie.'

Rebus was thinking back three years to their big push against Topper Hamilton: they'd set up surveillance, used a bit of pressure here and there, got a few people to talk. In the end, it hadn't so much amounted to a hill of beans as to a fart in an empty can. The procurator fiscal had decided not to proceed to trial. But then God or Fate, call it what you like, had provided a spin to the story. Not a plague of boils or anything for Topper Hamilton, but a nasty little

7

cancer which had given him more grief than the whole of the Lothian and Borders Police. He'd been in and out of hospital, endured chemo and the whole works, and had emerged a more slender figure in every sense.

The Farmer – who'd once settled an office argument by reeling off the books in both Old and New Testaments – wasn't yet content that God and life had done their worst to Topper, or that retribution had been meted out in some mysterious divine way. He wanted Topper in court, even if they had to wheel him there on a trolley.

It was a personal thing.

'Last time I looked,' Rebus said now, 'it wasn't illegal to invest in a casino.'

'It is if your name hasn't come up during the vetting procedure. Think Topper could get a gaming licence?'

'Fair point. But I still don't see –'

'Something else I heard. You've got a snitch works as a croupier.'

'So?'

'Same casino Topper has a finger in.'

Rebus saw it all and started shaking his head. 'I made him a promise. He'll tell me about punters, but nothing on the management.'

'And you'd rather keep that promise than give me a birthday present?'

'A relationship like that . . . it's eggshells.'

The Farmer's eyes narrowed. 'You think ours isn't? Talk to him, John. Get him to do some ferreting.'

'I could lose a good snitch.'

'Plenty more bigmouths out there.' The Farmer watched Rebus get to his feet. 'I was looking for you earlier. You were in the video room.'

'A missing person.'

'Suspicious?'

Rebus shrugged. 'Could be. He went up to the bar for a round of drinks, never came back.'

'We've all done that in our time.'

'His parents are worried.'

'How old is he?'

'Twenty-three.'

The Farmer thought about it. 'Then what's the problem?'

TWO

The problem was the past. A week before, he'd received a phone call from a ghost.

'Inspector John Rebus, please.'

'Speaking.'

'Oh, hello there. You probably won't remember me.' A short laugh. 'That used to be a bit of a joke at school.'

Rebus, immune to every kind of phone call, had this pegged a crank. 'Why's that?' he asked, wondering which punchline he was walking into.

'Because it's my name: Mee.' The caller spelt it for him. 'Brian Mee.'

Inside Rebus's head, a fuzzy photograph took sudden shape – a mouth full of prominent teeth, freckled nose and cheeks, a kitchen-stool haircut. 'Barney Mee?' he said.

More laughter on the line. 'Aye, they used to call me Barney. I'm not sure I ever knew why.'

Rebus could have told him: after Barney Rubble in *The Flintstones*. He could have added, because you were a dense wee bastard. But instead he asked how this ghost from his past was doing.

'No' bad, no' bad.' The laugh again; Rebus recognized it now as a sign of nerves.

'So what can I do for you, Brian?'

'Well, me and Janis, we thought ... Well, it was my mum's idea actually. She knew your dad. Both my mum and dad knew him, only my dad passed away, like. They all used to drink at the Goth.'

'Are you still in Bowhill?'

'Never quite escaped. Ach, it's all right really. I work in Glenrothes though. Lucky to have a job these days, eh? Mind, you've done well for yourself, Johnny. Do you still get called that?'

'I prefer John.'

'I remember you hated it when anyone called you Jock.' Another wheezing laugh. The photo was even sharper now, bordered with a white edge the way photos always were in the past. A decent footballer, a bit of a terrier, the hair reddish-brown. Dragging his satchel along the ground until the stitching rubbed away. Always with some huge hard sweet in his mouth, crunching down on it, his nose running. And one incident: he'd lifted some nude mags from under his dad's side of the bed and brought them to the toilets next to the Miners' Institute, there to be pored over like textbooks. Afterwards, half a dozen twelve-year-old boys had looked at each other, minds fizzing with questions.

'So what can I do for you, Brian?'

'Like I say, it was my mum's idea. Only, she remembered you were in the police in Edinburgh – saw your name in the paper a while back – and she thought you could maybe help.'

'With what?'

'Our son. I mean, mine and Janis's. He's called Damon.'

'What's he done?' Rebus thought: something minor, and way outside his territory anyway.

'He's vanished.'

'Run away?'

'More like in a puff of smoke. He was in this club with his pals, see, and he went—'

'Have you tried calling the police?' Rebus caught himself. 'I mean Fife Constabulary.'

'Oh aye.' Mee sounded dismissive. 'They asked a few questions, like, sniffed around a bit, then said there was nothing they could do. Damon's twenty-three. They say he's got a right to bugger off if he wants.'

'They've got a point. People run away all the time, Brian. Girl trouble maybe.'

'He was engaged.'

'Maybe he got scared?'

'Helen's a lovely girl. Never a raised voice between them.'

'Did he leave a note?'

'Nothing. I went through this with the police. He didn't take any clothes or anything. He didn't have any reason to go.'

'So you think something's happened to him?'

'I know what those buggers are thinking. They say we should give him another week or so to come back, or at least get in touch, but I know they'll only start doing something about it when the body turns up.'

Again, Rebus could have confirmed that this was only sensible. Again, he knew Mee wouldn't want to hear it.

'The thing is, Brian,' he said, 'I work in Edinburgh. Fife's not my patch. I mean, I can make a couple of phone calls, but it's hard to know what else to do.'

The voice was close to despair. 'Well, if you could just do *some*thing. Like, anything. We'd be very grateful. It would put our minds at rest.' A pause. 'My mum always speaks well of your dad. He's remembered in this town.'

And buried there, too, Rebus thought. He picked up a pen. 'Give me your phone number, Brian.' And, almost an afterthought, 'Better give me the address, too.'

That evening, he drove north out of Edinburgh, paid his toll at the Forth Bridge, and crossed into Fife. It wasn't as if he never went there – he had a brother in Kirkcaldy. But though they spoke on the phone every month or so, there were seldom visits. He couldn't think of any other family he still had in Fife. The place liked to call itself 'the Kingdom' and there were those who would agree that it was another country, a place with its own linguistic and cultural currency. For such a small place it seemed almost endlessly complex – had seemed that way to Rebus even when he was growing up. To outsiders the place meant coastal scenery and St Andrew's, or a stretch of motorway between Edinburgh and Dundee, but the west-central Fife of Rebus's childhood had been very different, ruled by coal mines and linoleum, dockyards and chemical plants, an industrial landscape shaped by basic needs, and producing people who were wary and inward-looking with the blackest humour you'd ever find.

They'd built new roads since Rebus's last visit, and knocked down a few more landmarks, but the place didn't feel so very different from thirty-odd years before. It wasn't such a great span of time after all, except in human terms; maybe not even then. Entering Cardenden – Bowhill had disappeared from road signs in the 1960s, even if locals still knew it as a village distinct from its neighbour – Rebus slowed to see if the memories would turn out sweet or sour. Then he caught sight of a Chinese takeaway and thought: both, of course.

Brian and Janis Mee's house was easy enough to find: they were standing by the gate waiting for him. Rebus had been born in a prefab but brought up in a house just like the one he now parked in front of. Brian Mee practically opened the car door for him, and was trying to shake his hand while Rebus was still emerging from his seat.

'Let the man catch his breath!' Janis Mee snapped.

She was still standing by the gate, arms folded. 'How have you been, Johnny?'

And Rebus realized that Brian Mee had married Janis Playfair, the only girl in his long and trouble-strewn life who'd ever managed to knock him unconscious.

The narrow, low-ceilinged living room was full to bursting – not just Rebus and Janis and Brian, but Brian's mother and Mr and Mrs Playfair. Introductions had to be made, and Rebus guided to 'the seat by the fire'. The room was overheated. A pot of tea was produced, and on the table by Rebus's armchair sat enough slices of cake to feed a football crowd.

'He's a brainy one,' Janis's mother said, handing Rebus a framed photo of Damon Mee. 'Plenty of certificates from school. Works hard. Saving up to get married. The date's set for next August.'

The photo showed a smiling imp, not long out of school. 'Have you got anything more recent?'

Janis handed him a packet of snapshots. 'From last summer.'

Rebus went through them slowly. It saved having to look at the faces around him. He felt like a doctor, expected to produce an immediate diagnosis and remedy. The photos showed a man in his early twenties, still retaining the impish smile but recognizably older. Not careworn exactly, but with something behind the eyes, some disenchantment with adulthood. A few of the photos showed Damon's parents.

'We all went together,' Brian explained. 'Janis's mum and dad, my mum, Helen and her parents.'

Beaches, a big white hotel, poolside games. 'Where is it?'

'Lanzarote,' Janis said, handing him his tea. In a few of the pictures she was wearing a bikini – good body for her age, or any age come to that. He tried not to linger.

'Can I keep a couple of the close-ups?' he asked. Janis looked at him. 'Of Damon.' She nodded and he put the other photos back in their packet.

'We're really grateful,' someone said. Janis's mum? Brian's? Rebus couldn't tell.

'Does Helen live locally?'

'Practically round the corner.'

'I'd like to talk to her.'

'I'll give her a bell,' Brian Mee said, leaping to his feet.

'Damon had been drinking in some club?'

'Guisers,' Janis said, handing round cigarettes. 'It's in Kirkcaldy.'

'On the Prom?'

She shook her head, looking just the same as she had that night of the school dance ... shaking her head, telling him so far and no further. 'In the town. It used to be a department store.'

'It's really called Gaitanos,' Mr Playfair said. Rebus remembered him, too. He was an old man now.

'Where does Damon work?' Careful to stick to the present tense.

Brian Mee came back into the room. 'Same place I do. I managed to get him a job in packaging. He's been learning the ropes; it'll be management soon.'

Working-class nepotism; jobs handed down from father to son. Rebus was surprised it still existed.

'Helen'll be here in a minute,' Brian added.

'Are you not eating any cake, Inspector?' said Mrs Playfair.

Helen Cousins hadn't been able to add much to Rebus's picture of Damon, and hadn't been there the night he'd vanished. But she'd introduced him to someone who had, Andy Peters. Andy had been part of the group at Gaitanos. There'd been four of them. They'd been in the same year at school and still met up once or twice a week, sometimes to watch Raith Rovers if the weather was decent and the mood took them, other times for an evening session in a pub or club. It was only their third or fourth visit to Guisers.

Rebus thought of paying the club a visit, but knew he should talk to the local cops first, and decided that it could all wait until morning. He knew he was jumping through hoops. He didn't expect to find anything the locals had missed. At best, he could reassure the family that everything possible had been done.

Next morning he made a few phone calls from his office, trying to find someone who could be bothered to answer some casual questions from an Edinburgh colleague. He had one ally – Detective Sergeant Hendry at Dunfermline CID – but only reached him at the third attempt. He asked Hendry for a favour, then put the phone down and got back to his own work. But it was hard to concentrate. He kept thinking about Bowhill and about Janis Mee, née Playfair. Which led him – eventually – guiltily – to thoughts of Damon. Younger runaways tended to take the same route: by bus or train or hitching, and to London, Newcastle, Edinburgh or Glasgow. There were organizations who would keep an eye open for runaways, and even if they wouldn't always reveal their whereabouts to the anxious families, at least they could confirm that someone was alive and unharmed.

But a twenty-three-year-old, someone a bit cannier and with money to hand ... could be anywhere. No destination was too distant – he owned a passport, and it hadn't turned up. Rebus knew, too, that Damon had a current account at the local bank, complete with cashcard, and an interest-bearing account with a building society in Kirkcaldy. The bank might be worth trying. Rebus picked up the telephone again.

The manager at first insisted that he'd need something in writing, but relented when Rebus promised to fax him later. Rebus held while the manager went off to check, and had doodled half a village, complete with stream, parkland and school, by the time the man came back.

'The most recent withdrawal was from a cash machine in Kirkcaldy. One hundred pounds on the twenty-second.'

'What time?'

'I've no way of knowing.'

'No other withdrawals since then?'

'No.'

'How up-to-date is that information?'

'Very. Of course a cheque – especially if post-dated – would take longer to show up.'

'Could you keep tabs on that account, let me know if anyone starts using it again?'

'I could, but I'd need it in writing, and I might also need Head Office approval.'

'Well, see what you can do, Mr Brayne.'

'It's Bain,' the bank manager said coldly, putting down the phone.

DS Hendry didn't get back to him until late afternoon.

'Gaitanos,' Hendry said. 'I don't know the place personally. Locals call it Guisers. It's a pretty choice establishment. Two stabbings last year, one inside the club itself, the other in the back alley where the owner parks his Merc. Local residents are always girning about the noise when the place lets out.'

'What's the owner's name?'

'Charles Mackenzie, nicknamed "Charmer". He seems to be clean. A couple of uniforms talked to him about Damon Mee, but there was nothing to tell. Know how many missing persons there are every year? They're not exactly a white-hot priority. God knows there are times I've felt like doing a runner myself.'

'Haven't we all? Did the woolly suits talk to anyone else at the club?'

'Such as?'

'Bar staff, punters.'

'No. Someone did take a look at the security video for the night Damon was there, but they didn't see anything.'

'Where's the video now?'

'Back with its rightful owner.'

'Am I going to be stepping on toes if I ask to see it?'

'I think I can cover you. I know you said this was personal, John, but why the interest?'

'I'm not sure I can explain.' There were words – community, history, memory – but Rebus didn't think they'd be enough.

'They mustn't be working you hard enough over there.'

'Just the twenty-four hours every day.'

THREE

Matty Paine could tell a few stories. He'd worked his way round the world as a croupier. Cruise liners he'd worked on, and in Nevada. He'd spent a couple of years in London, dealing out cards and spinning the wheel for some of the wealthiest in the land, faces you'd recognize from the TV and the papers. Moguls, royalty, stars – Matty had seen them all. But his best story – the one people sometimes disbelieved – was about the time he'd been recruited to work in a casino in Beirut. This was at the height of the civil war, bomb sites and rubble, smoke and charred buildings, refugees and regular bursts of small-arms fire. And amazingly, in the midst of it all (or, to be fair, on the edge of it all), a casino. Not exactly legal. Run from a hotel basement with torchlight when the generator failed and not much in the way of refreshments, but with no shortage of punters – cash bets, dollars only – and a management team of three who prowled the place like Dobermanns, since there was no sur-veillance and no other way to check that the games were being played honestly. One of them had stood next to Matty for a full forty minutes one session, making him sweat despite the air-conditioning. He'd reminded Matty of the gaffers casinos employed to check on apprentices. He knew the gaffers were there to protect *him* as much as the punters – there were professional gamblers out there who'd psych out a trainee, watch them for hours, whole nights and weeks, looking for the flaw that would give them an edge over the house. Like, when you were starting out, you didn't always vary the force with which you span the wheel, or sent the ball rolling, and if they could suss it, they'd get a pretty good idea which quadrant the ball was going to stop in. Good croupiers were immune to this. A really good croupier – one of a very select, very highly thought of group – could master the wheel and get the ball to land pretty well where *they* wanted.

Of course, this might be against the interests of the house, too. And in the end, that's why the checkers were out there, patrolling the tables. They were looking out for the house. In the end it all came down to the house.

And when things had got a wee bit too hot in London, Matty had come home, meaning Edinburgh, though really he was from Gullane – perhaps the only boy ever to be raised there and not show the slightest interest in golf. His father had played – his mother too, come to that. Maybe she still did; he didn't keep in touch. There had been an awkward moment at the casino when a neighbour from Gullane days, an old business friend of his father's, had turned up, a bit the worse for wear and in tow with three other middle-aged punters. The neighbour had glanced towards Matty from time to time, but had eventually shaken his head, unable to place the face.

'Does he know you?' one of the all-seeing gaffers had asked quietly, seeking out some scam against the house.

Matty had shaken his head. 'A neighbour from when I was growing up.' That was all; just a ghost from the past. He supposed his mother *was* still alive. He could probably find out by opening the phone book. But he wasn't that interested.

'Place your bets, please, ladies and gentlemen.'

Different houses had different styles. You either did your spiel in English or French. House rules changed, too. Matty's strengths were roulette and blackjack, but really he was happy in charge of any sort of game – most houses liked that he was flexible, it meant there was less chance of him trying some scam. It was the one-note wonders who tried small, stupid diddles. His latest employers seemed fairly laid back. They ran a clean casino which boasted only the very occasional high roller. Most of the punters were business people, well enough heeled but canny with it. You got husbands and wives coming in, proof of a relaxed atmosphere. There were younger punters too – a lot of those were Asians, mainly Chinese. The money they changed, according to the cashier, had a funny feel and smell to it.

'That's because they keep it in their underwear,' the day boss had told her.

The Asians ... whatever they were ... sometimes worked in local restaurants; you could smell the kitchen on their crumpled jackets and shirts. Fierce gamblers, no game was ever played quickly enough for their liking. They'd slap their chips down like they were in a playground betting game. And they talked a lot, almost never in English. The gaffers didn't like that, never could tell what they might be scheming. But their money was good, they seldom caused trouble, and they lost a percentage same as everyone else.

'Daft bastards,' the night manager said. 'Know what they do with a big win? Go bung it on the gee-gees. Where's the sense in that?'

Where indeed? No point giving your money to a bookmaker when the casino would happily take it instead.

It wasn't really on for croupiers to be friends with the clients, but sometimes it happened. And it couldn't very well not happen with Matty and Stevie Scoular, since they'd been in the same year at school. Not that they'd known one another well. Stevie had been the football genius, also more than fair at the hundred and two hundred metres, swimming and basketball. Matty, on the other hand, had skived off games whenever possible, forgetting to bring his kit or getting his mum to write him notes. He was good at a couple of subjects – maths and woodwork – but never sat beside Stevie in class. They even lived at opposite ends of the town.

At playtime and lunchtime, Matty ran a card game – three-card brag mostly, sometimes pontoon – playing for dinner money, pocket money, sweets and comics. A few of the cards were nicked at the corners, but the other players didn't seem to notice and Matty got a reputation as 'lucky'. He'd take bets on horse races too, sometimes passing the bets onto an older boy who wouldn't be turned away by the local bookmaker. Often though, Matty would simply pocket the money and if someone's horse happened to win, he'd say he couldn't get the bets on in time and hand back the stake.

He couldn't tell you exactly when it was that Stevie had started spending less breaktime dribbling past half a dozen despairing pairs of legs and more hanging around the edges of the card school. Thing about three-card brag, it doesn't take long to pick it up and even a moron can have a stab at playing. Soon enough, Stevie was losing his dinner money with the rest of them, and Matty's pockets were about bursting with loose change. Eventually, Stevie had seemed to see sense, drifted away from the game and back to keepie-up and dribbling. But he'd been hooked, no doubt about it. Maybe only for a few weeks, but a lot of those lunch-times had been spent cadging sweets and apple cores, the better to stave off hunger.

Even then, Matty had thought he'd be seeing Stevie again. It had just taken the best part of a decade, that was all.

When Stevie Scoular walked into the casino, people looked his way. It was the done thing. He was a sharp dresser, young, usually accompanied by women who looked like models. When Stevie had first walked into the Morvena, Matty's heart had sunk. They hadn't seen one another since school and here Stevie was, local boy made good, a hero, picture in the papers and plenty of money in the bank. Here was a schoolboy dream made flesh. And what was Matty? He had stories he could tell but that was about it. So he'd been hoping Stevie wouldn't grace his table, or if he did that he wouldn't recognize him. But Stevie had seen him, seemed to know him straight off and come bouncing up.

'Matty!'

'Hello there, Stevie.'

It was flattering really. Stevie hadn't become big-headed or anything. He took the whole thing – the way his life had gone – as a bit of a joke really. He'd made Matty promise to meet him for a drink when his shift was over. All through their conversation, Matty had been aware of gaffers hovering and when Stevie wandered off to another table one of them muttered in Matty's ear and another croupier took over from him.

He hadn't been in the plush back office that often, just for the initial interview and to discuss a couple of big losses on his table. The casino's owner, Mr Mandelson, was watching a football match on Sky Sports. He was well-built, mid-forties, his face pock-marked from childhood acne. His hair was black, slicked back from the forehead, long at the collar. He always seemed to know what he was about.

'How's the table tonight?' he asked.

'Look, Mr Mandelson, I know we're not supposed to be too friendly with the punters, but Stevie and me were at school together. Haven't clapped eyes on one another since – not till tonight.'

'Easy, Matty, easy.' Mandelson motioned for him to sit down. 'Something to drink?' A smile. 'No alcohol on shift, mind.'

'Ehh ... a Coke maybe.'

'Help yourself.'

There was a fridge in the far corner, stocked with white wine, champagne and soft drinks. A couple of the female croupiers said Mandelson had tried it on with them, plying them with booze. But he didn't seem upset by a refusal: they still had their jobs. There were seven female croupiers all told, and only two had spoken to Matty about it. It made him wonder about the other five.

He took a Coke and sat down again.

'So, you and Stevie Scoular, eh?'

'I haven't seen him in here before.'

'I think he only recently found out about the place. He's been in a few times, dropped some hefty bets.' Mandelson was staring at him. 'You and Stevie, eh?'

'Look, if you're worried, just take me off whatever table he's playing.'

'Nothing like that, Matty.' Mandelson's face broke into a grin. 'It's nice to have a friend, eh? Nice to meet up again after all these years. Don't you worry about anything. Stevie's the King of Edinburgh. As long as he keeps scoring goals, we're all his subjects.' He paused. 'Nice to know someone who knows the King, almost makes me feel like royalty myself. On you go now, Matty.'

Matty got up, leaving the Coke unopened.

'And don't you go upsetting that young man. We don't want to put him off his game, do we?'

FOUR

It had taken a couple of days to get the tape from Gaitanos. At first, they thought they'd wiped it, and then they'd sent the wrong day's recording. But at last Rebus had the right tape and had watched it at home half a dozen times before deciding he could use someone who knew what he was doing . . . and a video machine that would freeze-frame without the screen looking like a technical problem.

Now he'd seen all there was to see. He'd watched a young man cease to exist. Of course, Hendry was right, a lot of people disappeared every year. Sometimes they turned up again – dead or alive – and sometimes they didn't. What did it have to do with Rebus, beyond the promise to a family that he'd make sure the Fife police hadn't missed something? Maybe the pull wasn't Damon Mee, but Bowhill itself; and maybe even then, the Bowhill of his past rather than the town as it stood today.

He was working the Damon Mee case in his free time, which, since he was on day shift at St Leonard's, meant the evenings. He'd checked again with the bank – no money had been withdrawn from any machines since the twenty-second – and with Damon's building society. No money had been withdrawn from that account either. Even this wasn't unknown in the case of a runaway; sometimes they wanted to shed their whole history, which meant ditching their identity and everything that went with it. Rebus had passed a description of Matty to hostels and drop-in centres in Edinburgh, and faxed the same description to similar centres in Glasgow, Newcastle, Aberdeen and London. He'd also faxed details to the National Missing Persons Bureau in London. He checked with a colleague who knew about 'MisPers' that he'd done about all he could.

'Not far off it,' she confirmed. 'It's like looking for a needle in a haystack without knowing which field to start with.'

'How big a problem is it?'

She puffed out her cheeks. 'Last figures I saw were for the whole of Britain. I think there are around 25,000 a year. Those are the *reported* MisPers. You can add a few thousand for the ones nobody notices. There's a nice distinction actually: if nobody knows you're missing, are you really missing?'

Afterwards, Rebus telephoned Janis Mee and told her she might think about running up some flyers and putting them up in positions of prominence in nearby towns, maybe even handing them out to Saturday shoppers or evening drinkers in Kirkcaldy. A photo of

Damon, a brief physical description, and what he was wearing the night he left. She said she'd already thought of doing so, but that it made his disappearance seem so final. Then she broke down and cried and John Rebus, thirty-odd miles away, asked if she wanted him to 'drop by'.

'I'll be all right,' she said.

'Sure?'

'Well...'

Rebus reasoned that he was going to go to Fife anyway. He had to drop the tape back to Gaitanos, and wanted to see the club when it was lively. He'd take the photos of Damon with him and show them around. He'd ask about the candyfloss blonde. The technician who had worked with the videotape had transferred a still to his computer and managed to boost the quality. Rebus had some hard copies in his pocket. Maybe other people who'd been queuing at the bar would remember something.

Maybe.

His first stop, however, was the cemetery. He didn't have any flowers to put on his parents' grave, but he crouched beside it, fingers touching the grass. The inscription was simple, just names and dates really, and underneath, 'Not Dead, But at Rest in the Arms of the Lord'. He wasn't sure whose idea that had been, not his certainly. The headstone's carved lettering was inlaid with gold, but it had already faded from his mother's name. He touched the surface of the marble, expecting it to be cold, but finding a residual warmth there. A blackbird nearby was trying to worry food from the ground. Rebus wished it luck.

By the time he reached Janis's, Brian was home from work. Rebus told them what he'd done so far, after which Brian nodded, apologized, and said he had a Burns Club meeting. The two men shook hands. When the door closed, Janis and Rebus exchanged a look and then a smile.

'I see that bruise finally faded,' she said.

Rebus rubbed his right cheek. 'It was a hell of a punch.'

'Funny how strong you can get when you're angry.'

'Sorry.'

She laughed. 'Bit late to apologize.'

'It was just...'

'It was everything,' she said. 'Summer holidays coming up, all of us leaving school, you going off to join the army. The last school dance before all of that. That's what it was.' She paused. 'Do you know what happened to Mitch?' She watched Rebus shake his head. 'Last I heard,' she said, 'he was living somewhere down south. The two of you used to be so close.'

'Yes.'

She laughed again. 'Johnny, it was a long time ago, don't look so solemn.' She paused. 'I've sometimes wondered ... ach, not for years, but just now and then I used to wonder what would have happened...'

'If you hadn't punched me?'

She nodded. 'If we'd stayed together. Well, you can't turn the clock back, eh?'

'Would the world be any better if we could?'

She stared at the window, not really seeing it. 'Damon would still be here,' she said quietly. A tear escaped her eye, and she fussed for a handkerchief in her pocket. Rebus got up and made towards her. Then the front door opened, and he retreated.

'My mum,' Janis smiled. 'She usually pops in around this time. It's like a railway station around here, hard to find any privacy.'

Then Mrs Playfair walked into the living room.

'Hello, Inspector, thought that was your car. Is there any news?'

'I'm afraid not,' Rebus said. Janis got to her feet and hugged her mother, the crying starting afresh.

'There there, pet,' Mrs Playfair said quietly. 'There there.'

Rebus walked past the two of them without saying a word.

It was still early when he reached Gaitanos. He had a word with one of the bouncers, who was keeping warm in the lobby until things started getting busy, and the man lumbered off to fetch Charles Mackenzie, *aka* Charmer. It seemed strange to Rebus: here he was, standing in the very foyer he'd stared at for so long on the video monitor. The camera was high up in one corner with nothing to show whether it was working.

Rebus gave it a wave anyway. If he disappeared tonight, it could be his farewell to the world.

'Inspector Rebus.' They'd spoken on the phone. The man who came forward to shake Rebus's hand stood about five feet four and was as thin as a cocktail glass. Rebus placed him in his mid-fifties. He wore a powder-blue suit and an open-necked white shirt with suntan and gold jewellery beneath. His hair was silver and thinning, but as well-cut as the suit. 'Come through to the office.'

Rebus followed Mackenzie down a carpeted corridor to a gloss-black door with a sign on it saying 'Private'. There was no door handle. Mackenzie unlocked the door and motioned for Rebus to go in.

'After you, sir,' Rebus said. You never knew what could be waiting behind a locked door.

What greeted Rebus this time was an office which seemed to double as a broom-cupboard. Mops and a vacuum cleaner rested against one wall. A bank of screens spread across three filing cabinets showed what was happening inside and outside the club. Unlike the video Rebus had watched, these screens each showed a certain location.

'Are these recording?' Rebus asked. Mackenzie shook his head.

'We've got a roaming monitor, and that's the only recording we get. But this way, if we spot trouble anywhere, we can watch it unfold.'

'Like that knifing in the alley?'

'Messed up my Mercedes.'

'So I heard. Is that when you called the police? When your car stopped being a bystander?'

Mackenzie laughed and wagged a finger, but didn't answer. Rebus couldn't see where he'd earned his nickname. The guy had all the charm of sandpaper.

'I brought back your video.' Rebus placed it on the desk.

'All right to record over it now?'

'I suppose so.' Rebus handed over the computer-enhanced photograph. 'The missing person is slightly right of centre, second row.'

'Is that his doll?'

'Do you know her?'

'Wish I did.'

'You haven't seen her before.'

'She doesn't look the sort I'd forget.'

Rebus took back the picture. 'Mind if I show this around?'

'The place is practically empty.'

'I thought I might stick around.'

Mackenzie frowned and studied the backs of his hands. 'Well, you know, it's not that I don't want to help or anything...'

'But?'

'Well, it's hardly conducive to a party atmosphere, is it? That's our slogan – "The best party of your life, every night!" – and I don't think a police officer mooching around asking questions is going to add to the ambience.'

'I quite understand, Mr Mackenzie. I was being

thoughtless.' Mackenzie lifted his hands, palms towards Rebus: no problem, the hands were saying.

'And you're quite right,' Rebus continued. 'In fact, I'd be a lot quicker if I had some assistance – say, a dozen uniforms. That way, I wouldn't be "mooching around" for nearly so long. In fact, let's make it a couple of dozen. We'll be in and out, quick as a virgin's first poke. Mind if I use your phone?'

'Whoah, wait a minute. Look, all I was saying was ... Look, how much do you want?'

'Sorry, sir?'

Mackenzie reached into a desk drawer, lifted out a brick of twenties, pulled about five notes free. 'Will this do it?'

Rebus sat back. 'Am I to understand you're trying to offer me a cash incentive to leave the premises?'

'Whatever. Just slope off, eh?'

Rebus stood up. 'To me, Mr Mackenzie, that's an open invitation to stay.'

So he stayed.

The looks he got from staff made him feel like a football fan trapped on the opposition's turf. The way they all shook their heads as soon as he held up the photo, he knew word had gone around. He had a little more luck with the punters. A couple of lads had seen the woman before.

'Last week, was it?' one asked the other. 'Maybe the week before.'

'Not long ago anyway,' the other agreed. 'Cracker, isn't she?'

'Has she been in since?'

'Haven't seen her. Just that one night. Didn't quite get the nerve up to ask for a dance.'

'Was she with anyone?'

'No idea.'

They didn't recognize Damon Mee though. They said they never paid much attention to blokes.

'We're not that way inclined, sweetie.'

The place was still only half full, but the bass was loud enough to make Rebus feel queasy. He managed to order an orange juice at the bar and just sat there, looking at the photo. The woman interested him. The way her head was angled, the way her mouth was open, she could have been saying something to Damon. A minute later, he was gone. Had she said she'd meet him somewhere? Had something happened at that meeting? He'd shown the photo to Damon's mates from that night. They remembered seeing her, but swore Damon hadn't introduced himself.

'She seemed sort of cold,' one of them had said. 'You know, like she wanted to be left alone.'

Rebus had studied the video again, watched her progress towards the bar, showing no apparent interest in Damon's leaving. But then she'd turned and started pushing her way back through the throng, no drink to show for her long wait.

At midnight exactly, she'd left the nightclub. The final shot was of her turning left along the pavement, watched by a few people who were waiting to get in.

And now Charles Mackenzie wanted to give Rebus money.

At three quid for an orange juice, maybe he should have taken it.

If the place had been heaving, maybe he wouldn't have noticed them.

He was finishing his second drink and trying not to feel like a leper in a children's ward when he recognized one of the doormen. There was another man with him, tall and fat and pale. His idea of clubbing was probably the connection of baseball bat to skull. The bouncer was pointing Rebus out to him. Here we go, Rebus thought. They've brought in the professionals. The fat man said something to the bouncer, and they both retreated to the foyer, leaving Rebus with an empty glass and only one good reason to order another drink.

Get it over with, he thought, sliding from his bar stool and walking around the dance floor. There was always the fire exit, but it led on to the alley and, if they were waiting for him there, the only witness would be Mackenzie's Mercedes. He wanted things kept as public as possible. The street outside would be busy, no shortage of onlookers and possible good Samaritans. Or at the very least, someone to call for an ambulance.

He paused in the foyer and saw that the bouncer was back at his post on the front door. No sign of the fat man. Then he glanced along the corridor towards

Mackenzie's office, and saw the fat man planted outside the door. He had his arms folded in front of him and wasn't going anywhere.

Rebus walked outside. The air had seldom tasted so good. He tried to calm himself with a few deep breaths. There was a car parked at the kerbside, a gold-coloured Rolls-Royce, with nobody in the driver's seat. Rebus wasn't the only one admiring the car, but he was probably alone in memorizing its number plate.

He moved his own car to where he could see the Roller, then sat tight. Half an hour later, the fat man emerged, looking to left and right. He walked to the car, unlocked it and held open the back door. Only now did another figure emerge from the club. Rebus caught a swishing full-length black coat, sleek hair and chiselled face. The man slipped into the car, and the fat man closed the door and squeezed in behind the steering wheel.

Like them or not, you had to admire Rollers. They carried tonnage.

FIVE

Back in Edinburgh he parked his car and sat in it, smoking his eleventh cigarette of the day. He sometimes played this game with himself – I'll have one more tonight, and deduct one from tomorrow's allowance. Or he would argue that any cigarette after midnight came from the next day's stash. He'd lost count along the way, but reckoned by now he should be going whole days without a ciggie to balance the books. Well, when it came down to it, ten cigarettes a day or twelve, thirteen, fourteen – what difference did it make?

The street he was parked on was quiet. Residential for the most part with big houses. There was a basement bar on the corner, but it did mostly lunchtime business from the offices on neighbouring streets. By ten, the place was usually locked up. Taxis rippled past him and the occasional drunk, hands in pockets, would weave slowly homewards. A few of the taxis stopped just in front of him and disgorged their fares, who would then climb half a dozen steps and push open the door to the Morvena Casino. Rebus had never been inside the place. He placed the occasional bet on the horses, but that was about it. Gave up doing the football pools. He bought a National Lottery ticket when opportunity arose, but often didn't get round to checking the numbers. He had half a dozen tickets lying around, any one of which could be his fortune. He quite liked the notion that he might have won a million and not know it; preferred it, in fact, to the idea of actually having the million in his bank account. What would he do with a million pounds? Same as he'd do with fifty thou – self-destruct.

Only faster.

Janis had asked him about Mitch – Roy Mitchell, Rebus's best friend at school. The more time Rebus had spent with her, the less he'd seen of Mitch. They'd been going to join the army together, hoping they might get the same regiment. Until Mitch lost his eye. That had been the end of that. The army hadn't wanted him any more. Rebus had headed off, sent Mitch a couple of letters, but by the time his first leave came, Mitch had already left Bowhill. Rebus had stopped writing after that...

When the Morvena's door opened next, it was so eight or nine young people could leave. The shift changeover. Three of them turned one way, the rest another. Rebus watched the group of three. At the first set of lights, two kept going and one crossed the road and took a left. Rebus started his engine and followed. When the lights turned green, he signalled left and sounded his horn, then pulled the car over and wound down his window.

'Mr Rebus,' the young man said.

'Hello, Matty. Let's go for a drive.'

Officers from other cities, people Rebus met from time to time, would remark on how cushy he had it in Edinburgh. Such a beautiful place, and prosperous. So little crime. They thought to be dangerous a city had to look dangerous. London, Manchester, Liverpool – these places were dangerous in their eyes. Not Edinburgh, not this sleepy walking-tour with its monuments and museums. Tourism aside, the life-blood of the city was its commerce, and Edinburgh's commerce – banking, insurance and the like – was discreet. The city hid its secrets well, and its vices too. Potentially troublesome elements had been moved to the sprawling council estates which ringed the capital, and any crimes committed behind the thick stone walls of the city centre's tenements and houses were often muffled by those same walls. Which was why every good detective needed his contacts.

Rebus took them on a circuit – Canonmills to Ferry Road, back up to Comely Bank and through Stock-bridge into the New Town again. And they talked.

'I know we had a sort of gentleman's agreement, Matty,' Rebus said.

'But I'm about to find out you're no gentleman?'

Rebus smiled. 'You're ahead of me.'

'I wondered how long it would take.' Matty paused,

stared through the windscreen. 'You know I'll say no.'

'Will you?'

'I said at the start, no ratting on anyone I work with or work for. Just the punters.'

'Not even many of them. It's not like I've been milking you, Matty. I'll bet you've dozens of stories you haven't told me.'

'I work tables, Mr Rebus. People don't place a bet and then start yacking about some job they've pulled or some scam they're running.'

'No, but they meet friends. They have a drink, get mellow. It's a relaxing place, so I've heard. And maybe then they talk.'

'I've not held anything back.'

'Matty, Matty.' Rebus shook his head. 'It's funny, I was just thinking tonight about that night we met. Do you remember?'

How could he forget? A couple of drinks after work, a car borrowed from a friend who was away on holiday. Matty hadn't been back long. Driving through the town was great, especially with a buzz on. Streets glistening after the rain. Late night, mostly taxis for company. He just drove and drove and, as the streets grew quieter, he pushed the accelerator a bit further, caught a string of green lights, then saw one turning red. He didn't know how good the tyres were, imagined braking hard and skidding in the wet. Fuck it, he put his foot down.

Just missed the cyclist. The guy was coming through on green and had to twist his front wheel hard to avoid contact, then teetered and fell onto the road. Matty's foot eased off the accelerator, thought about the brake, then went back on the accelerator again.

That's when he saw the cop car. And thought: I can't afford this.

They'd breathalysed him and taken him to St Leonard's, where he'd sat around and let the machinery chew him up. Would it come to a trial? Would there be a report in the papers? How could he keep his name from getting around? He'd worked himself up into a right state by the time Detective Inspector John Rebus had sat down across from him.

'I can't afford this,' Matty had blurted out.

'Sorry?'

He'd swallowed and tried to find a story. 'I work in a casino. Any black mark against me, they'll boot me out. Look, if it's a question of compensation or anything ... like, I'll buy him a new bike.'

Rebus had picked up a sheet of paper. 'Drunk driving ... in a borrowed car you weren't insured to drive ... running a red light ... leaving the scene of an accident ...' Rebus had shaken his head, read the sheet through one more time and then put it down, and looked up at Matty. 'What casino did you say you work for?'

Later, he'd given Matty two business cards, both with his phone number. 'The first one's for you to tear up in disgust,' he'd said. 'The other one's to keep. Have we got a deal?'

'Look, Mr Rebus,' Matty said now, as the car stopped for lights on Raeburn Place, 'I'm doing the best I can.'

'I want to know what's happening behind the scenes at the Morvena.'

'I wouldn't know.'

'Anything at all, it doesn't matter how small it seems. Any stories, gossip, anything overheard. Ever seen the owner entertain people in his office? Maybe open the place for a private party? Names, faces, anything at all. Put your mind to it, Matty. Just put your mind to it.'

'They'd skin me alive.'

'Who's they?'

Matty swallowed. 'Mr Mandelson.'

'He's the owner, right?'

'Right.'

'On paper at least. What I need to know is who might be pulling his strings.'

'I can't see anyone pulling his strings.'

'You'd be surprised. Hard bastard, is he?'

'I'd say so.'

'Given you grief?' Matty shook his head. 'Do you see much of him?'

'Not much,' Matty said. Not, he might have added, until recently at any rate.

Rebus dropped him at the foot of Broughton Street, headed back up to Leith Walk and along York Place onto Queen Street. He passed the casino again and slowed, a frown on his face. At the next set of lights, he did a U-turn so he could be sure. Yes, it was the Roller from Gaitanos, no doubt about it.

Parked outside the Morvena.

SIX

'Mind if I join you?'

Rebus was eating breakfast in the canteen and wishing there was more caffeine in the coffee, or more coffee in the coffee come to that. He nodded to the empty chair and Siobhan sat down.

'Heavy night?' she said.

'Believe it or not, I was on orange juice.'

She bit into her muffin, washing it down with milk. 'Harry tells me you had him working a tape.'

'Harry?'

'Our video wizard. He said it was a missing person. News to me.'

'It's not official. The son of an old schoolfriend of mine.'

'Standing at a bar one minute and gone the next?' Rebus looked at her and she smiled. 'Harry's a great one for gossip.'

'I'm working on it in my own time.'

'Need any help?'

'Handy with a crystal ball, are you?' But Rebus dug

into his pocket and brought out the still from the video. 'That's Damon there,' he said, pointing.

'Who's that with him?'

'I wish I knew. She's not with him. I don't know who she is.'

'You've asked around?'

'I was at the club last night. A few punters remembered her.'

'Male punters?' She waited till Rebus nodded. 'You were asking the wrong sex. Any man would have given her the once-over, but only superficially. A woman, on the other hand, would have seen her as competition. Have you never noticed women in nightclubs? They've got eyes like lasers. Plus, what if she visited the loo?'

Rebus was interested now. 'What if she did?'

'*That's* where women talk. Maybe someone spoke to her, maybe she said something back. Ears would have been listening.' Siobhan stared at the photo. 'Funny, it's almost like she's got an aura.'

'How do you mean?'

'Like she's shining.'

'Interior light.'

'Exactly.'

'No, that's what your friend Harry said. It's the interior lighting that gives that effect.'

'Maybe he didn't know what he was saying.'

'I'm not sure I know what *you're* saying.'

'Some religions believe in spirit guides. They're supposed to lead you to the next world.'

47

'You mean this one's not the end?'

She smiled. 'Depends on your religion.'

'Well, it's plenty enough for me.' He looked at the photo again.

'I was sort of joking, you know, about her being a spirit guide.'

'I know.'

He met with Helen Cousins that night. They spoke over a drink in the Auld Hoose. Rebus hadn't been in the place in quarter of a century, and there'd been changes. They'd installed a pool table.

'You weren't invited along that night?' Rebus asked her.

She shook her head. She was twenty, three years younger than Damon. The fingers of her right hand played with her engagement ring, rolling it, sliding it off over the knuckle and then back down again. She had short, lifeless brown hair, dark, tired eyes, and acne around her mouth.

'I was out with the girls. See, that was how we played it. One night a week the boys would go off on their own, and we'd go somewhere else. Then another night we'd all get together.'

'Do you know anyone who was at Gaitanos that night? Apart from Damon and his pals?'

She chewed her bottom lip while considering. The ring came off her finger and bounced once before hitting the floor. She stooped to pick it up.

'It's always doing that.'

'You better watch it, you're going to lose it.'

She pushed the ring back on. 'Yes,' she said, 'Corinne and Jacky were there.'

'Corinne and Jacky?' She nodded. 'Where can I find them?'

A phone call brought them to the Auld Hoose. Rebus got in the round: Bacardi and Coke for Corinne, Bacardi and blackcurrant for Jacky, a second vodka and orange for Helen and another bottle of no-alcohol lager for himself. He eyed the optics behind the bar. His mean little drink was costing more than a whisky. Something was telling him to indulge in a Teacher's. Maybe it's my spirit guide, he thought, dismissing the idea.

Corinne had long black hair crimped with curling tongs. Her pal Jacky was tiny, with dyed platinum hair. When he got back to the table, they were in a huddle, exchanging gossip. Rebus took out the photograph again.

'Look,' Corinne said, 'there's Damon.' So they all had a good look. Then Rebus touched his finger to the strapless aura.

'Remember her?'

Helen prickled visibly. 'Who is she?'

'Yeah, she was there,' Jacky said.

'Was she with anyone?'

'Didn't see her up dancing.'

'Isn't that why people go to clubs?'

'Well, it's one reason.' All three broke into a giggle.

'You didn't speak to her?'

'No.'

'Not even in the toilets?'

'I saw her in there,' Corinne said. 'She was doing her eyes.'

'Did she say anything?'

'She seemed sort of ... stuck-up.'

'Snobby,' Jacky agreed.

Rebus tried to think of another question and couldn't. They ignored him for a while as they exchanged news. It was like they hadn't seen each other in a year. At one point, Helen got up to use the toilet. Rebus expected the other two to accompany her, but only Corinne did so. He sat with Jacky for a moment, then, for want of anything else to say, asked her what she thought of Damon. He meant about Damon disappearing, but she didn't take it that way.

'Ach, he's all right.'

'Just all right?'

'Well, you know, Damon's heart's in the right place, but he's a bit thick. A bit slow, I mean.'

'Really?' The impression Rebus had received from Damon's family had been of a genius in waiting. He suddenly realized just how superficial his own portrait of Damon was. Siobhan's words should have been warning – so far he'd heard only one side of Damon. 'Helen likes him though?'

'I suppose so.'

'They're engaged.'

'It happens, doesn't it? I've got friends who got engaged just so they could throw a party.' She looked around the bar, then leant towards him. 'They used to have some mega arguments.'

'What about?'

'Jealousy, I suppose. She'd see him notice someone, or he'd say she'd been letting some guy chat her up. Just the usual.' She turned the photo around so it faced her. 'She looks like a dream, doesn't she? I remember she was dressed to kill. Made the rest of us spit.'

'But you'd never seen her before?'

Jacky shook her head. No, no one seemed to have seen her before, nobody knew who she was. Unlikely then that she was local.

'Were there any buses in that night?'

'That doesn't happen at Gaitanos,' she told him. 'It's not "in" enough any more. There's a new place in Dunfermline. That gets the busloads.' Jacky tapped the photo. 'You think she's gone off with Damon?'

Rebus looked at her and saw behind the eyeliner to a sharp intelligence. 'It's possible,' he said quietly.

'I don't think so,' she said. 'She wouldn't be interested, and he wouldn't have had the guts.'

On his way home, Rebus dropped into St Leonard's. The amount he was paying in bridge tolls, he was thinking about a season ticket. There was a fax on his desk. He'd been promised it in the afternoon, but there'd been a delay. It identified the owner of the Rolls-Royce as a Mr Richard Mandelson, with an address in Juniper Green. Mr Mandelson had no criminal record outstanding, whether for motoring offences or anything else. Rebus tried to imagine some poor parking warden trying to give the Roller a ticket with the fat man behind the wheel. There were a few more facts about Mr Mandelson, including last known occupation.

Casino manager.

SEVEN

Matty and Stevie Scoular saw one another socially now. Stevie would sometimes phone and invite Matty to some party or dinner, or just for a drink. At the same time as Matty was flattered, he did wonder what Stevie's angle was, had even come out and asked him.

'I mean,' he'd said, 'I'm just a toe-rag from the school playground, and you ... well, you're SuperStevie, you're the king.'

'Aye, if you believe the papers.' Stevie had finished his drink – Perrier, he had a game the next day. 'I don't know, Matty, maybe it's that I miss all that.'

'All what?'

'Schooldays. It was a laugh back then, wasn't it?'

Matty had frowned, not really remembering. 'But the life you've got now, Stevie, man. People would kill for it.'

And Stevie had nodded, looking suddenly sad.

Another time, a couple of kids had asked Stevie for his autograph, then had turned and asked Matty for his, thinking that whoever he was, he had to be somebody. Stevie had laughed at that, said something about it being a lesson in humility. Again, Matty didn't get it. There were times when Stevie seemed to be on a different planet. Maybe it was understandable, the pressure he was under. Stevie seemed to remember a lot more about school than Matty did: teachers' names, the lot. They talked about Gullane, too, what a boring place to grow up. Sometimes they didn't talk much at all. Just took out a couple of dolls: Stevie would always bring one along for Matty. She wouldn't be quite as gorgeous as Stevie's, but that was all right. Matty could understand that. He was soaking it all up, enjoying it while it lasted. He had half an idea that Stevie and him would be best friends for life, and another that Stevie would dump him soon and find some other distraction. He thought Stevie needed him right now much more than *he* needed Stevie. So he soaked up what he could, started filing the stories away for future use, tweaking them here and there ...

Tonight they took in a couple of bars, a bit of a drive in Stevie's Beamer: he preferred BMWs to Porsches, more space for passengers. They ended up at a club, but didn't stay long. Stevie had a game the next day. He was always very conscientious that way: Perrier and early nights. Stevie dropped Matty off outside his flat, sounding the horn as he roared away. Matty hadn't spotted the other car, but he heard a door opening, looked across the road and recognized Malibu straight off. Malibu was Mr Mandelson's driver. He'd eased himself out of the Roller and was holding open the back door while looking over to Matty.

So Matty crossed the street. As he did so, he walked into Malibu's shadow, cast by the sodium street lamp. At that moment, though he didn't know what was about to happen, he realized he was lost.

'Get in, Matty.'

The voice, of course, was Mandelson's. Matty got into the car and Malibu closed the door after him, then kept guard outside. They weren't going anywhere.

'Ever been in a Roller before, Matty?'

'I don't think so.'

'You'd remember if you had. I could have had one years back, but only by buying secondhand. I wanted to wait until I had the cash for a nice new one. That leather smell – you don't get it with any other car.' Mandelson lit a cigar. The windows were closed and the car started filling with sour smoke. 'Know how I came to afford a brand new Roller, Matty?'

'Hard work?' Matty's mouth was dry. Cars, he thought: Rebus's, Stevie's, and now this one. Plus, of course, the one he'd borrowed that night, the one that had brought him to this.

'Don't be stupid. My dad worked thirty years in a shop, six days a week and he still couldn't have made the down-payment. Faith, Matty, that's the key. You have to believe in yourself, and sometimes you have to trust other people – strangers some of them, or people you don't like, people it's hard to trust. That's the gamble life's making with you, and if you place your bet, sometimes you get lucky. Except it's not luck – not entirely. See, there are odds, like in every game, and that's where judgment comes in. I like to think I'm a good judge of character.'

Only now did Mandelson turn to look at him. There seemed to Matty to be nothing behind the eyes, nothing at all.

'Yes, sir,' he said, for want of anything better.

'That was Stevie dropped you off, eh?' Matty nodded. 'Now, your man Stevie, he's got something else, something we haven't discussed yet. He's got a gift. He's had to work, of course, but the thing was there to begin with. Don't ask me where it came from or why it should have been given to him in particular – that's one for the philosophers, and I don't claim to be a philosopher. What I am is a businessman ... and a gambler. Only I don't bet on nags or dogs or a turn of the cards, I bet on people. I'm betting on you, Matty.'

'Me?'

Mandelson nodded, barely visible inside the cloud of smoke. 'I want you to talk to Stevie on my behalf. I want you to get him to do me a favour.'

Matty rubbed his forehead with his fingers. He knew what was coming but didn't want to hear it.

'I saw a recent interview,' Mandelson went on, 'where he told the reporter he always gave a hundred and ten per cent. All I want is to knock maybe twenty per cent off for next Saturday's game. You know what I'm saying?'

Next Saturday ... An away tie at Kirkcaldy. Stevie

expected to run rings around the Raith Rovers defence.

'He won't do it,' Matty said. 'Come to that, neither will I.'

'No?' Mandelson laughed. A hand landed on Matty's thigh. 'You fucked up in London, son. They knew you'd end up taking a croupier's job somewhere else, it's the only thing you know how to do. So they phoned around, and eventually they phoned *me*. I told them I'd never heard of you. That can change, Matty. Want me to talk to them again?'

'I'd tell them you lied to them the first time.'

Mandelson shrugged. 'I can live with that. But what do you think they'll do to *you*, Matty? They were pretty angry about whatever scheme it was you pulled. I'd say they were furious.'

Matty felt like he was going to heave. He was sweating, his lungs toxic. 'He won't do it,' he said again.

'Be persuasive, Matty. You're his friend. Remind him that his tab's up to three and a half. All he has to do is ease off for one game, and the tab's history. And Matty, I'll know if you've talked to him or not, so no games, eh? Or you might find yourself with no place left to hide.'

EIGHT

Rebus searched his flat, but came up with only half a dozen snapshots: two of his ex-wife Rhona, posing with Samantha, their daughter, back when Sammy was seven or eight; two further shots of Sammy in her teens; one showing his father as a young man, kissing the woman who would become Rebus's mother; and a final photograph, a family grouping, showing uncles, aunts and cousins whose names Rebus didn't know. There were other photographs, of course – at least, there had been – but not here, not in the flat. He guessed Rhona still kept some, maybe his brother Michael had the others. But they could be anywhere. Rebus hadn't thought of himself as the kind to spend long nights with the family album, using it as a crutch to memory, always with the fear that remembrance would yield to sentiment.

If I died tonight, he thought, what would I bequeath to the world? Looking around, the answer was: nothing. The thought scared him, and worst of all it made him want a drink, and not just one drink but a dozen.

Instead of which, he drove north back into Fife. It had been overcast all day, and the evening was warm. He didn't know what he was doing, knew he had precious little to say to either of Damon's parents, and yet that's where he ended up. He'd had the destination in mind all along.

Brian Mee answered the door, wearing a smart suit and just finishing knotting his tie.

'Sorry, Brian,' Rebus said. 'Are you off out?'

'In ten minutes. Come in anyway. Is it Damon?'

Rebus shook his head and saw the tension in Brian's face turn to relief. Yes, a visit in person wouldn't be good news, would it? Good news had to be given immediately by telephone, not by a knock at the door. Rebus should have realized; he'd been the bearer of bad news often enough in his time.

'Sorry, Brian,' he repeated. They were in the hallway. Janis's voice came from above, asking who it was.

'It's Johnny,' her husband called back. Then to Rebus, 'It's all right to call you that?'

'Of course. It's my name, isn't it?' He could have added: again, after all this time. He looked at Brian, remembering the way they'd sometimes mistreated him at school: not that 'Barney' had seemed to mind, but who could tell for sure? And then that night of the last school dance ... Brian had been there for Mitch. Brian had been there; Rebus had not. He'd been too busy losing Janis, and losing consciousness.

She was coming downstairs now. 'I'll be back in a sec,' Brian said, heading up past her.

'You look terrific,' Rebus told her. The blue dress was well-chosen, her make-up highlighting all the right features of her busy face. She managed a smile.

'No news?'

'Sorry,' he said again. 'Just thought I'd see how you are.'

'Oh, we're pining away.' Another smile, tinged by shame this time. 'It's a dinner-dance, we bought the tickets months back. It's for the Jolly Beggars.'

'Nobody expects you to sit at home every night, Janis.'

'But all the same ...' Her cheeks grew flushed and her eyes sought his. 'We're not going to find him, are we?'

'Not easily. Our best bet's that he'll get in touch.'

'If he can,' she said quietly.

'Come on, Janis.' He put his hands on her shoulders, like they were strangers and about to dance. 'You might hear from him tomorrow, or it might take months.'

'And meantime life goes on, eh?'

'Something like that.'

She smiled again, blinking back tears. 'Why don't you come with us, John?'

Rebus dropped his hands from her shoulders. 'I haven't danced in years.'

'So you'd be rusty.'

'Thanks, Janis, but not tonight.'

'Know something? I bet they play the same records we used to dance to at school.'

It was his turn to smile. Brian was coming back downstairs, patting his hair into place.

'You'd be welcome to join us, Johnny,' he said.

'I've another appointment, Brian. Maybe next time, eh?'

'Let's make that a promise.'

They went out to their cars together. Janis pecked him on the cheek, Brian shook his hand. He watched them drive off then headed to the cemetery.

It was dark, and the gates were locked, so Rebus sat in his car and smoked a cigarette. He thought about his parents and the rest of his family and remembered stories about Bowhill, stories which seemed inextricable from family history: mining tragedies; a girl found drowned in the River Ore; a holiday car crash which had erased an entire family. Then there was Johnny Thomson, Celtic goalkeeper, injured during an 'Old Firm' match. He was in his early twenties when he died, and was buried behind those gates, not far from Rebus's parents. *Not Dead, But at Rest in the Arms of the Lord.*

The Lord had to be a bodybuilder.

From family he turned to friends and tried recalling a dozen names to put to faces he remembered from schooldays. Other friends: people he'd known in the army, the SAS. All the people he'd dealt with during his career in the police. Villains he'd put away, some who'd slipped through his fingers. People he'd interviewed, suspected, questioned, broken the worst kind of news to. Acquaintances from the Oxford Bar and all the other pubs where he'd ever been a regular. Local shopkeepers. Jesus, the list was endless. All these people who'd played a part in his life, in shaping who he was and how he acted, how he felt about things. All of them, out there somewhere and nowhere, gathered together only inside his head. And chief among them tonight, Brian and Janis.

That night of the school dance ... It was true he'd been drunk – elated. He'd felt he could *do* anything, *be* anything. Because he'd come to a decision that day – he wouldn't join the army, he'd stay in Bowhill with Janis, apply for a job at the dockyard. His dad had told him not to be so stupid – 'short-sighted' was the word he'd used. But what did parents know about their children's desires? So he'd drunk some beer and headed off to the dance, his thoughts only of Janis. Tonight he'd tell her. And Mitch, of course. He'd have to tell Mitch, tell him he'd be heading into the army alone. But Mitch wouldn't mind, he'd understand, as best friends had to.

But while Rebus had been outside with Janis, his friend Mitch was being cornered by four teenagers who considered themselves his enemies. This was their last chance for revenge, and they'd gone in hard, kicking and punching. Four against one ... until Barney had waded in, shrugging off blows, and dragged Mitch to safety. But one kick had done the damage, dislodging a retina. Mitch's vision stayed fuzzy in that eye for a few days, then disappeared. And where had Rebus been? Out cold on the concrete by the bike sheds.

And why had he never thanked Barney Mee?

He blinked now and sniffed, wondering if he was coming down with a cold. He'd had this idea when he came back to Bowhill that the place would seem beyond redemption, that he'd be able to tell himself it had lost its sense of community, become just another town for him to pass through. Maybe he'd wanted to put it behind him. Well, it hadn't worked. He got out of the car and looked around. The street was dead. He reached up and hauled himself over the iron railings and walked a circuit of the cemetery for an hour or so, and felt strangely at peace.

NINE

'So what's the panic, Matty?'

After a home draw with Rangers, Stevie was ready for a night on the town. One-one, and of course he'd scored his team's only goal. The reporters would be busy filing their copy, saying for the umpteenth time that he was his side's hero, that without him they were a very ordinary team indeed. Rangers had known that: Stevie's marker had been out for blood, sliding studs-first into tackles which Stevie had done his damnedest to avoid. He'd come out of the game with a couple of fresh bruises and grazes, a nick on one knee but, to his manager's all too palpable relief, fit to play again midweek.

'I said what's the panic?'

Matty had worried himself sleepless. He knew he had several options. Speak to Stevie, that was one of them. Another was not to speak to him, but tell Mandelson he had. Then it would be down to whether or not Mandelson believed him. Option three: do a runner; only Mandelson was right about that – he was running out of places to hide. With *two* casino bosses out for his blood, how could he ever pick up another croupier's job?

If he spoke with Stevie, he'd lose a new-found friend. But to stay silent ... well, there was very little percentage in it. So here he was in Stevie's flat, having demanded to see him. In the corner, a TV was replaying a tape of the afternoon's match. There was no commentary, just the sounds of the terraces and the dug-outs.

'No panic,' he said now, playing for time.

Stevie stared at him. 'You all right? Want a drink or something?'

'Maybe a vodka.'

'Anything in it?'

'I'll take it as it comes.'

Stevie poured him a drink. Matty had been here half an hour now, and they still hadn't talked. The telephone had hardly stopped: reporters' questions, family and friends offering congratulations. Stevie had shrugged off the superlatives.

Matty took the drink, swallowed it, wondering if he could still walk away. Then he remembered Malibu, and saw shadows falling.

'Thing is, Stevie,' he said. 'You know my boss at the Morvena, Mr Mandelson?'

'I owe him money, of course I know him.'

'He says we could do something about that.'

'What? My tab?' Stevie was checking himself in the

mirror, having changed into his on-the-town clothes. 'I don't get it,' he said.

Well, Stevie, Matty thought, it was nice knowing you, pal. 'All you have to do is ease off next Saturday.'

Stevie frowned and turned from the mirror. 'Away to Raith?' He came and sat down opposite Matty. 'He told you to tell me?' He waited till Matty nodded. 'That bastard. What's in it for him?'

Matty wriggled on the leather sofa. 'I've been thinking about it. Raith are going through a bad patch, but you know yourself that if you're taken out of the equation...'

'Then they'd be up against not very much. My boss has told everybody to get the ball to me. If they spend the whole game doing that and I don't do anything with it...'

Matty nodded. 'What I think is, the odds will be on you scoring. Nobody'll be expecting Raith to put one in the net.'

'So Mandelson's cash will be on a goalless draw?'

'And he'll get odds, spread a lot of small bets around...'

'Bastard,' Stevie said again. 'How did he get you into this, Matty?'

Matty shifted again. 'Something I did in London.'

'Secrets, eh? Hard things to keep.' Stevie got up, went to the mirror again, and just stood there, hands by his sides, staring into it. There was no emotion in his voice when he spoke.

'Tell him he can fuck himself.'

Matty had to choke out the words. 'You sure that's the message?'

'Cheerio, Matty.'

Matty rose shakily to his feet. 'What am I going to do?'

'Cheerio, Matty.'

Stevie was as still as a statue as Matty walked to the door and let himself out.

Mandelson sat at his desk, playing with a Cartier pen he'd taken from a punter that day. The man was overdue on a payment. The pen was by way of a gift.

'So?' he asked Matty.

Matty sat on the chair and licked his lips. There was no offer of a drink today; this was just business. Malibu stood by the door. Matty took a deep breath – the last act of a drowning man.

'It's on,' he said.

Mandelson looked up at him. 'Stevie went for it?'

'Eventually,' Matty said.

'You're sure?'

'As sure as I can be.'

'Well, that better be watertight, or you might find yourself going for a swim with heavy legs. Know what I mean?'

Matty held the dark gaze and nodded.

Mandelson glanced towards Malibu, both of them were smiling. Then he picked up the telephone. 'You know, Matty,' he said, pushing numbers. 'I'm doing

you a favour. You're doing *yourself* a favour.' He
listened to the receiver. 'Mr Hamilton, please.' Then,
to Matty, 'See, what you're doing here is saving your
job. I overstretched myself, Matty. I wouldn't like that
to get around, but I'm trusting you. If this comes off –
and it better – then you've earned that trust.' He
tapped the receiver. 'It wasn't all my own money
either. But this will keep the Morvena alive and kicking.' He motioned for Matty to leave. Malibu tapped
his shoulder as an incentive.

'Topper?' Mandelson was saying as Matty left the
room. 'It's locked up. How much are you in for?'

Matty bided his time and waited till his shift was
over. He walked out of the smart New Town building
like a latterday Lazarus, and found the nearest pay-
phone, then had to fumble through all the rubbish in
his pockets, stuff that must have meant something
once upon a time, until he found the card.

The card with a phone number on it.

The following Saturday, Stevie Scoular scored his
team's only goal in their 1–0 win over Raith Rovers,
and Mandelson sat alone in his office, his eyes on the
Teletext results.

His hand rested on the telephone receiver. He was
expecting a call from Topper Hamilton. He couldn't
seem to stop blinking, like there was a grain of sand
in either eye. He buzzed the reception desk, told them
to tell Malibu he was wanted. Mandelson didn't know
how much time he had, but he knew he would make

it count. A word with Stevie Scoular, see if Matty really *had* put the proposition to him. Then Matty himself ... Matty was a definite, no matter what. Matty was about to be put out of the game.

The knock at the door had to be Malibu. Mandelson barked for him to come in. But when the door opened, two strangers sauntered in like they owned the place. Mandelson sat back in his chair, hands on the desk. He was almost relieved when they introduced themselves as police officers.

'I'm Detective Inspector Rebus,' the younger one said, 'this is Chief Superintendent Watson.'

'And you've come about the Benevolent Fund, right?'

Rebus sat down unasked, his eyes drifting to the TV screen and the results posted there. 'Looks like you just lost a packet. I'm sorry to hear it. Did Topper take a beating, too?'

Mandelson made fists of his hands. 'That wee bastard!'

Rebus was shaking his head. 'Matty did his best, only there was something he didn't know. Seems you didn't know either. Topper will be doubly disappointed.'

'What?'

Farmer Watson, still standing, provided the answer. 'Ever heard of Big Ger Cafferty?'

Mandelson nodded. 'He's been in Barlinnie a while.'

'Used to be the biggest gangster on the east coast. Probably still is. And he's a fan of Stevie's, gets videotapes of all his games. He almost sends him love letters.'

Mandelson frowned. 'So?'

'So Stevie's covered,' Rebus said. 'Try fucking with him, you're asking Big Ger to bend over. Your little proposal has probably already made it back to Cafferty.'

Mandelson swallowed and felt suddenly dry-mouthed.

'There was no way Stevie was going to throw that game,' Rebus said quietly.

'Matty ...' Mandelson choked the sentence off.

'Told you it was fixed? He was scared turdless, what else was he going to say? But Matty's *mine*. You don't touch him.'

'Not that you'd get the chance,' the Farmer added. 'Not with Topper *and* Cafferty after your blood. Malibu will be a big help, the way he took off five minutes ago in the Roller.' Watson walked up to the desk, looming over Mandelson like a mountain. 'You've got two choices, son. You can talk, or you can run.'

'You've got nothing.'

'I saw you that night at Gaitanos,' Rebus said. 'If you're going to lay out big bets, where better than Fife? Optimistic Raith fans might have bet on a goalless draw. You got Charmer Mackenzie to place the bets locally, spreading them around. That way it looked less suspicious.'

Which was why Mackenzie had wanted Rebus out

of there, whatever the price: he'd been about to do some business . . .

'Besides,' Rebus continued, 'when it comes down to it, what choice do you have?'

'You either talk to us . . .' the Farmer said.

'Or you disappear. People do it all the time.'

And it never stops, Rebus could have added. Because it's part of the dance – shifting partners, people you shared the floor with, it all changed. And it only ended when you disappeared from the hall.

And sometimes . . . sometimes, it didn't even end there.

'All right,' Mandelson said at last, the way they'd known he would, all colour gone from his face, his voice hollow, 'what do you want to know?'

'Let's start with Topper Hamilton,' the Farmer said, sounding like a kid unwrapping his birthday present.

It was Wednesday morning when Rebus got the phone call from a Mr Bain. It took him a moment to place the name: Damon's bank manager.

'Yes, Mr Bain, what can I do for you?'

'Damon Mee, Inspector. You wanted us to keep an eye on any transactions.'

Rebus leant forward in his chair. 'That's right.'

'There've been two withdrawals from cash machines, both in central London.'

Rebus grabbed a pen. 'Where exactly?'

'Tottenham Court Road was three days ago: fifty

pounds. Next day, it was Finsbury Park, same amount.'

Fifty pounds a day: enough to live on, enough to pay for a cheap bed and breakfast and two extra meals.

'How much is left in the account, Mr Bain?'

'A little under six hundred pounds.'

Enough for twelve days. There were several ways it could go. Damon could get himself a job. Or when the money ran out he could try begging. Or he could return home. Rebus thanked Bain and telephoned Janis.

'John,' she said, 'we got a postcard this morning.'

A postcard saying Damon was in London and doing fine. A postcard of apology for any fright he'd given them. A postcard saying he needed some time to 'get my head straight.' A postcard which ended 'See you soon.' The picture on the front was of a pair of breasts painted with Union Jacks.

'Brian thinks we should go down there,' Janis said. 'Try to find him.'

Rebus thought of how many B&Bs there'd be in Finsbury Park. 'You might just chase him away,' he warned. 'He's doing OK, Janis.'

'But why did he do it, John? I mean, is it something *we* did?'

New questions and fears had replaced the old ones. Rebus didn't know what to tell her. He wasn't family and couldn't begin to answer her question. Didn't *want* to begin to answer it.

'He's doing OK,' he repeated. 'Just give him some time.'

She was crying now, softly. He imagined her with head bowed, hair falling over the telephone receiver.

'We did everything, John. You can't know how much we've given him. We always put ourselves second, never a minute's thought for anything but him...'

'Janis...' he began.

She took a deep breath. 'Will you come and see me, John?'

Rebus looked around the office, eyes resting eventually on his own desk and the paperwork stacked there.

'I can't, Janis. I'd like to, but I just can't. See, it's not as if I...'

He didn't know how he was going to finish the sentence, but it didn't matter. She'd put her phone down. He sat back in his chair and remembered dancing with her, how brittle her body had seemed. But that had been half a lifetime ago. They'd made so many choices since. It was time to let the past go. Siobhan Clarke was at her desk. She was looking at him. Then she mimed the drinking of a cup of coffee, and he nodded and got to his feet.

Did a little dance as he shuffled towards her.

AFTERWORD

I wrote this novella a couple of years ago at the behest of my friend Otto Penzler. The theme of 'vanishing' has stayed with me ever since, to the extent that I have, in Raymond Chandler's phrase, 'cannibalized' part of it for a sub-plot in the subsequent full-length Rebus novel, *Dead Souls*, while altering the histories of the characters involved so that both can be read independently.